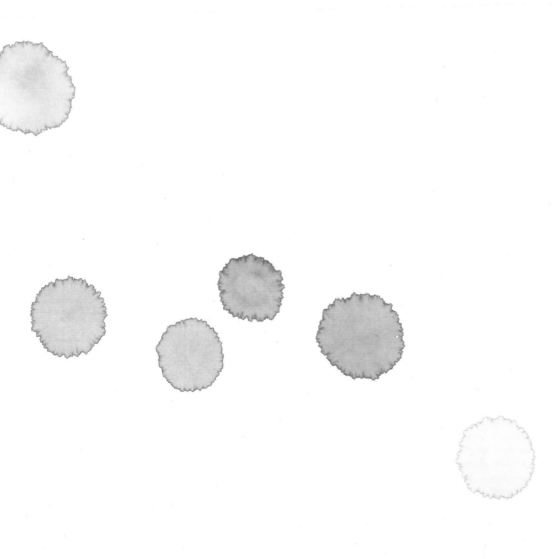

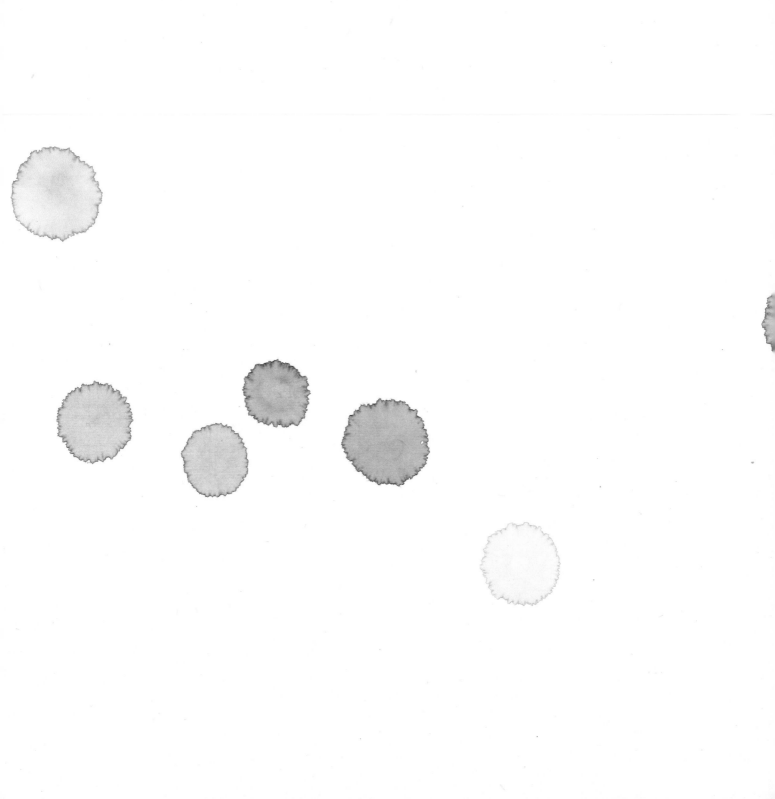

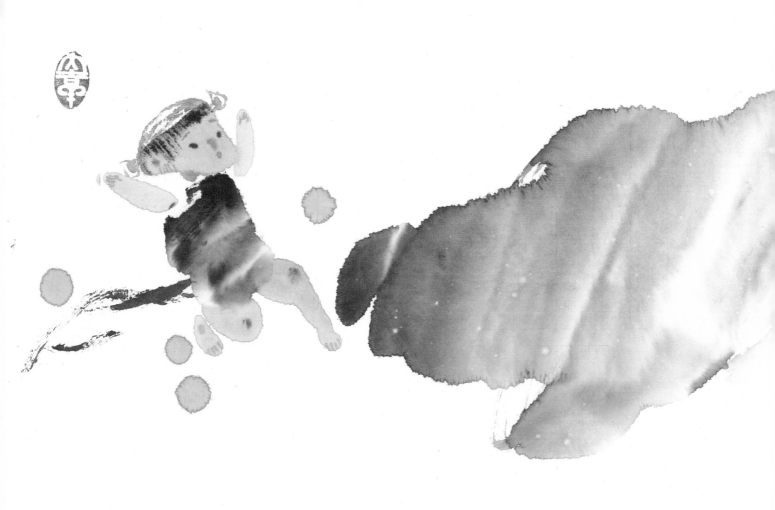

The Story of
Ink and Water

Illustrations by
Peilong Liang

Original text by Qingye Li

Translated and adapted by Chun Zhang

balestierpress

A long, long time ago, there was a sparkling little river, whose clear waters tinkled like a song. In this river lived the smart and spirited Water Girl. Her chubby body was soft and her skin was translucent.

She and the river animals bathed together every day,
splish-splashing around playing games.
Of course, it was Water Girl who won every time.

One day, Water Girl sighed. "Humph, we play in the water every
day. I'm tired of it, it's boring!"
A cockerel who happened to be walking by overheard this. "Come
with me to the river bank, it's beautiful over there," he suggested.
Water Girl blinked at him curiously. "Really?"

Water Girl arrived at the bank, and she found everything new and exciting. She spotted another child in the distance and happily ran up to him. He was covered head to toe in a shiny coat of black.

"Wow, who is this kid black as coal?" Water Girl teased.

The child politely answered, "I am Ink Boy, what's your name?"

"Me?" Water Girl said brightly, with her head held high. "I'm the beautiful Water Girl."

9

The sun hung high in the sky. It was either from the heat or because Ink Boy was nervous, that beads of sweat drip-dropped uncontrollably from his face. As Water Girl saw this, she felt slightly sorry for him and changed to a friendlier tone.

"Why don't you come to my place for a bath?"

Ink Boy jumped into the river with excitement, happily washing himself. Oh no! The dark coat flowed off from his body and suddenly the clear waters turned pitch black.

Water Girl watched this happen and burst into tears. Knowing that he caused trouble, Ink Boy climbed back up to the bank in a panic, still dripping wet. His face was full of embarrassment.

"Don't cry, black-coloured water has its own use."

Everyone turned around to look at who was speaking. It was a very strange little person who looked like a paintbrush and had a soft brush tip as his feet.

"This is Brush Boy," the wise cockerel introduced. It was only then that Water Girl stopped crying.

"Watch this!"

Brush Boy placed a sheet of paper on the ground, and after stretching out his feet to dip into the dark water, stood on his toes and began to dance gracefully on the paper.

One moment he stood upright, drawing thin lines under his feet. The next moment he leant back, dragging his body across the paper to make large, wide strokes with light to dark tones.

14

Under his dance steps, ink marks of all shades appeared on the paper. Everyone watched on in wonder.

"Look, it's a cat!" Water Girl cried excitedly.

Suddenly, an odd thing happened. The cat leapt out of the paper and started to miaow at the crowd. They were all stunned, they could not believe their eyes.

"Wow! That's amazing! Let me have a try!" said Water Girl.

Copying the movements of Brush Boy, she also began to dance on the paper.

The crowd stared as pretty layers of water marks emerged. Just as Water Girl was giggling with pride, these marks suddenly vanished without a trace.

"What happened?" Water Girl asked, full of confusion.

"Because your water had no ink in it, when the water dried, the marks disappeared. If you want to make a beautiful painting, both water and ink must be used," explained Brush Boy.

"I heard that ink is made up of five colours," the cockerel could not help but add.

"Yes, ink does have five colours," Brush Boy continued. "The amount of water in the brush affects how dark the colour becomes. A lot of water and a little ink makes a light colour, whereas a lot of ink and a little water makes a dark, sometimes even scorched black colour."

Everyone wanted to see the different colours of ink.

"Let's try one with lots of water and a little ink!" Water Girl impatiently suggested.

"Ok!" Smiling, Brush Boy dipped himself in the darkened river water and danced all over the paper again.

"A lamb! It's a lamb!" the cockerel cheered, pointing at the picture.

Brush Boy furrowed his brows. He appeared not fully satisfied with the painting.

18   "Something is missing."

Water Girl stared at the picture thoughtfully. "Maybe if the lamb had little bits of wool, it would look even better."

Brush Boy was struck by this idea. He jumped next to Ink Boy, dipped into the dark black ink, returned to the paper, and danced around. Flick flick flick - the lamb on the paper became clearer and clearer, and by the end they could even see tufts of wool!

"Amazing! It's like magic!" They were all open-mouthed in astonishment.

At this moment, the little lamb puffed out of the paper, running nimbly.

"So it seems it is only by using both dark and light ink that we can create beautiful pictures!"

"Now make one with a lot of ink and just a little water!" everyone insisted.

Brush Boy happily dipped into the ink, and once again bounced onto the paper. Dark ink, light ink, scorched black ink – Brush Boy continued to change the amounts of ink and water, revealing different layers of brush strokes. The next moment, a lifelike cow was born.

"Moo! Moo!" The cow walked out from the picture, looking as big as a real cow. Ink Boy was so excited, he did not realise he had such magical powers! He joyfully leapt towards the cow and climbed onto its back, cheering.

The longer the sun was out the hotter it became. Everyone started to drip with sweat. Water Girl came up with a bright idea. "Brush Boy, why don't you paint some clouds to hide the sun!"

"You smart alec, come with me!" Just as he
finished his sentence, Brush Boy lifted Water
Girl up to the sky and flew away.

Water Girl felt her body get lighter and lighter. Her playmates appeared further and further away, and the trees and mountains and all that was beautiful whizzed by below. She felt like a hovering bird, gently and joyfully blending into the blue sky.

Just then, Brush Boy pushed Water Girl forward, and all of a sudden a dazzling group of clouds appeared. Brush Boy leapt onto the clouds, stepping and rubbing on them with his ink-stained feet. The white clouds instantly turned into black ones. These black clouds gradually gathered together, every now and then flashing bolts of lightning.

"It's raining! How refreshing!" As Water Girl watched the rain pit-pattering down, she faintly heard the cheers of her playmates in the distance.

Not long after, the clouds drifted away and the rain stopped. The thick clusters of clouds spread: some turned into long, flat fishes, others into elephants rolling around. "Did those splish-splashing raindrops hide away in the clouds? Are they playing hide and seek with us, these ever-changing clouds?" thought Water Girl.

She stretched out her hand to try and grab the fluffy, cotton candy-like cloud, but nothing was there...

Suddenly, a hand appeared through the
clouds and softly grabbed hold of Water Girl.
She looked up, and lo and behold, the cloud
had turned into a beautiful maiden!

Water Girl was overwhelmed with excitement, and held tightly onto the Cloud Maiden. Together, they whooshed high and low through the skies. Not knowing how long they had been flying for, she looked down and could vaguely see her playmates waving at her, realising that she herself was moving closer and closer to them.

The Cloud Maiden smiled and brought out a precious gift. "These are pigments extracted from plants and minerals. I hope you can use them to create even more beautiful and colourful paintings!" she said. "Hooray!" everyone jumped with joy.

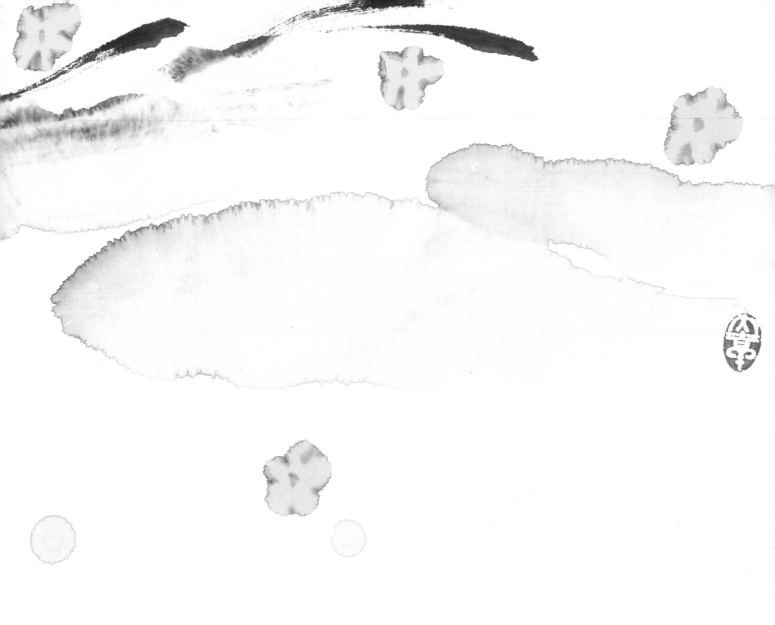

It was at this moment that they realised
Brush Boy was nowhere to be seen.
"Is he still playing around in the sky?"
they guessed.

"Wait, look!"
The Cloud Maiden waved her hand,
and out popped from her sleeve none
other than Brush Boy!

The Cloud Maiden patted Water Girl's head and paused meaningfully. "When ink and water are together, they can create all manner of paint effects. But without the brush or the paper, you still cannot paint anything." Ashamed, Water Girl said, "I used to be so sure of myself, always thinking I was the best. But actually, it's only by working together than we can do even greater things." Everyone began to cheer and clap at her words.

From that day on, Water, Ink, Brush and Paper were
often seen together, and the 'ink and water' paintings they
created became the symbols of traditional Chinese art.

Chinese painting is one of the oldest painting traditions in the world. It involves simple but effective tools, known as the 'four treasures.' They are: brush, ink, ink stone, and paper.

The brush usually has a bamboo handle and a brush tip made from animal hairs. When wet with ink, the hairs become very soft which makes it very easy to move around on the paper.

Ink is made from soot mixed with animal glue and then squashed to make a dry cake. The ink becomes a liquid by grinding the ink cake with water on an ink stone. Chinese painters have a particular love of black ink. They sometimes use coloured inks, but almost always use black ink.

Artists love the smooth and soft *xuan* paper for painting on. The name comes from the city of Xuancheng in the eastern Chinese province of Anhui, where the best paper is made from blue sandalwood bark and a small amount of rice straw. The moment the wet brush is applied, the ink soaks into the paper.

Chinese artists still continue to use this traditional technique to paint the world around them. The importance of water and ink is why traditional Chinese painting is simply named *shui mo hua* (水 墨 画), which literally means water and ink painting.

Balestier Press
71-75 Shelton Street, London WC2H 9JQ
www.balestier.com

The Story of Ink and Water
Originally published in Chinese as 水与墨的故事

Illustrations copyright © 2013 by Peilong Liang
Original Chinese text copyright © 2013 by Qingye Li
English translation and Introduction copyright © 2018 by Chun Zhang

First published in English by Balestier Press in 2018

ISBN 978 1 911221 07 4

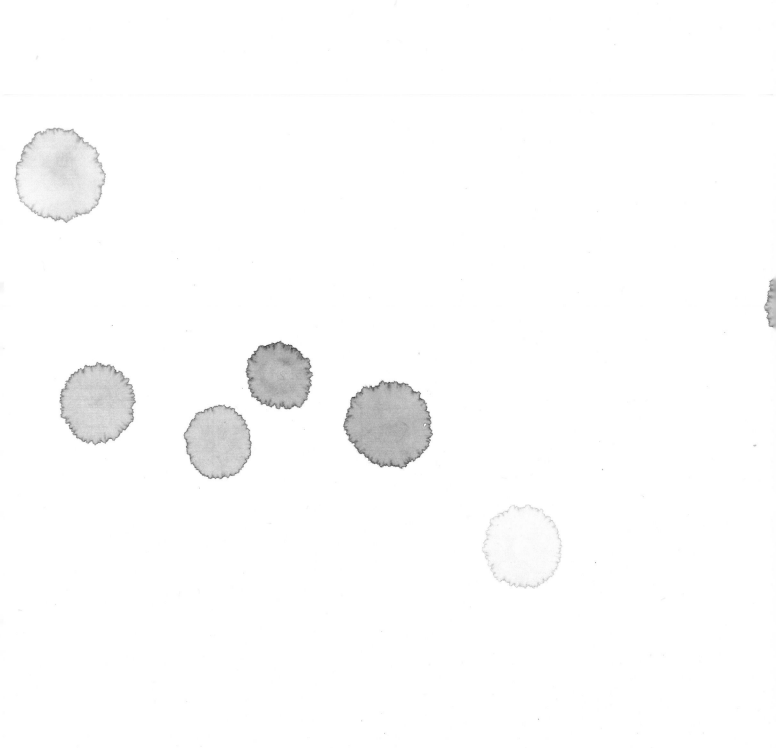